This book belongs to

....

Published by **Lion Cub Books**
www.spckpublishing.co.uk
Part of the SPCK Group
SPCK, Studio 101, The Record Hall,
16-16A Baldwin's Gardens, London EC1N 7RJ

ISBN 978-1-915748-07-2

First edition 2024
10 9 8 7 6 5 4 3 2 1

Acknowledgments
Psalm 121 on p.28–29 is taken from The Holy Bible, New International Version® NIV®
Copyright © 1973 1978 1984 2011 by Biblica, Inc. TM
Used by permission. All rights reserved worldwide.
A catalogue record for this book is available from the British Library
Produced on paper from sustainable sources
Printed and bound in China, November 2023 by Dream Colour (Hong Kong) Printing Limited

Good Night
Prayers for
Bedtime

lion cub
books

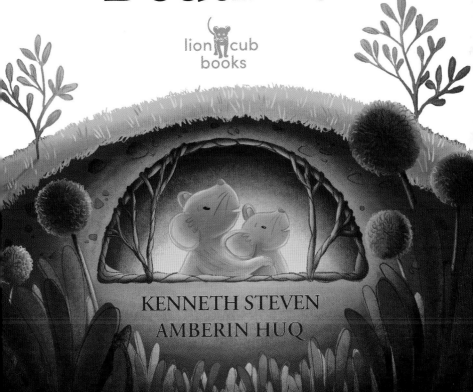

KENNETH STEVEN
AMBERIN HUQ

We whisper our prayer of
thanks for this day –
bless our sleeping tonight,
Father God.

Contents

At the End
of the Day

Dear God, the day that you made is now ending,
the light is beginning to fade.
Slowly the sounds are all falling silent
as everyone gets ready for rest.

We whisper our prayer of thanks for this day –
bless our sleeping tonight, Father God.

Soon now the stars you created will be starting to show,
shining out their fires in the dark;
the moon will climb high and stand still
like a silver balloon in the sky, as you watch over us.

We whisper our prayer of thanks for this day —
bless our sleeping tonight, Father God.

We think of the creatures gone to hide in their dens
keep them warm and safe as they dream just like us.
Thank you for making them all so amazing;
we ask you to watch over and care for each one.

We whisper our prayer
of thanks for this day —
bless our sleeping tonight,
Father God.

Dear God, thank you for our families,
who love and guide us through each day.
Watch over our friends who we share and play with;
may any quarrels be put behind us.

We whisper our prayer of thanks for this day –
bless our sleeping tonight, Father God.

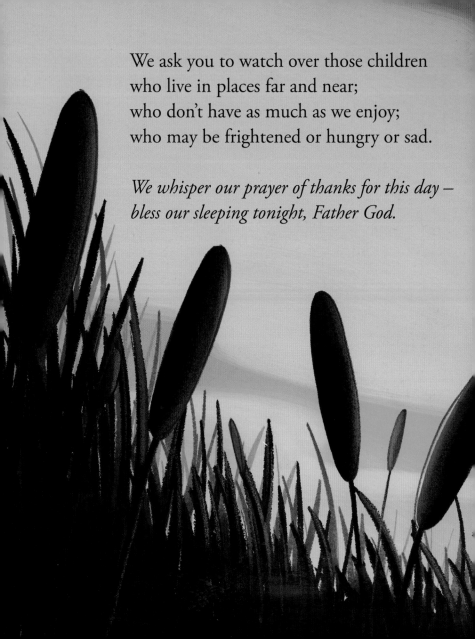

We ask you to watch over those children
who live in places far and near;
who don't have as much as we enjoy;
who may be frightened or hungry or sad.

*We whisper our prayer of thanks for this day —
bless our sleeping tonight, Father God.*

Help us remember, to never forget,
how you made our whole world to be good;
to see those who need you, to be kind and to care,
just as Jesus came to teach us to do.

We whisper our prayer of thanks for this day –
bless our sleeping tonight, Father God.

For Tomorrow

Dear God, tomorrow is a gift from you
that comes like a box
left at our door each new day;
inside are surprises and secrets and stories
wrapped up in ribbons, all ready to find.

We whisper our prayer of thanks for this day –
bless our sleeping tonight, Father God.

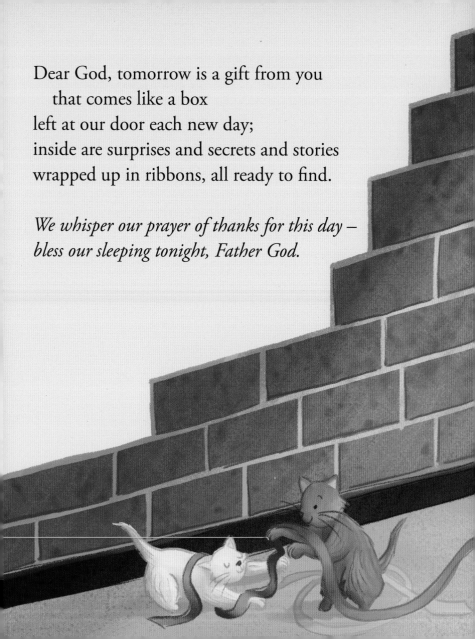

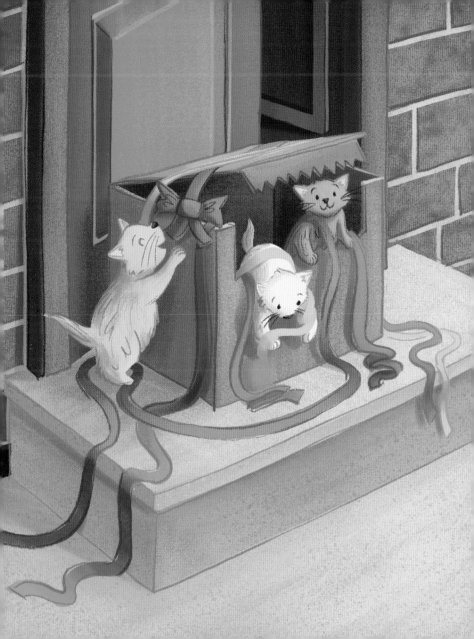

For each day is different the whole of our lives,
as you watch us grow and find out a bit more each day.
Then help us, dear God, to keep safe what we learn
in a place somewhere deep in our hearts.

We whisper our prayer of thanks for this day —
bless our sleeping tonight, Father God.

These Prayers
are Inspired by
Psalm 121

I lift up my eyes to the mountains –
where does my help come from?
My help comes from the Lord,
the Maker of heaven and earth.

He will not let your foot slip –
he who watches over you will not slumber;
indeed, he who watches over Israel
will neither slumber nor sleep.

The Lord watches over you –
the Lord is your shade at your right hand;
the sun will not harm you by day,
nor the moon by night.

The Lord will keep you from all harm –
he will watch over your life;
the Lord will watch over your coming and
going both now and forevermore.

My
Good Night
Prayer

_____

_____

_____

_____

_____